Conjoined: The Story of Rex and Roxanne—
The World's First Androgynous Siamese Twins

A Fictive Memoir by Larry W. Bryant

Foreword by Linda R. Backman, Ed.D.

Larry W Bryant

10 OCT 14

BookLocker.com, Inc.
2010

DEDICATION

For Gretchen B. Condon, whose spiritual conjoinment with
her father knows no bounds.

Table of Contents

Foreword

The prologue to Larry W. Bryant's first novella, *Conjoined*, spells out key components of core learning absolutely necessary for each of us to envelop with our hearts and minds. It is high time we **knew**, rather than suspected, that we arrive into incarnation at the moment of birth's first breath, holding a contract in our "hands" containing various elements of prenatal choice. The souls who are our family members, our type of body, and physical/mental capability are among the available choices we make in concert with the loving spiritual guidance we receive before arriving into a new lifetime.

For seventeen years it has been my blessing to guide soul regression clients into past lives, as well as into the time between our lives, when we are pure, pristine spirit energy. The light of core truth shines brightly for innumerable clients, as they realize that each lifetime, or incarnation, is preplanned. Once our life begins, free will perpetually exists for us to alter any aspect of our pre-birth contract. In conference with our spiritual team of guides and teachers, our life trajectory is developed with intention, prior to opening our eyes on this planet.

No incarnation is purposeless. Quite the contrary. As we travel our journey toward higher wisdom, soul development is ongoing, gaining depth, breadth, and height with each lifetime. We progress as an individual soul entity, along with contributing to the greater whole of the new humanity.

Rex and Roxanne are a shining example of the yin and yang of soul balance. The outer circle, representing the container of yin and yang, is the whole of soul interrelationship.

Within the circle are two fish-like representations of equal halves. A small portion, or dot, of the complementary energy of the partner lies inside each fish. What is the purpose of such intentional balance of yin and yang? The dance of two separate, yet uncommonly familiar, souls has been brought to light in thousands of unprompted soul regression cases, explaining that the vast majority of us have shared more lifetimes with one other soul. Such is the yin and yang of soul relatedness with your partner soul. Life contracts with your partner soul may lead to wondrous, fulfillment by interacting and supporting one another. On the other hand, the script of each life may intend for partner souls to "push each other's buttons," in order to enhance the advancement of one or both souls.

Apparently, Rex and Roxy created a complex pre-birth agreement, in defiance of societal norms, to provide potential learning to those with whom they would come into contact demonstrating that interrelationship can, and often does, serve equally as the partners carry out simultaneous roles of both puppeteer and puppet.

Bryant's hypothetical twins shed light on a crucial awareness I strongly believe all of us must gain. It would appear on the surface that one twin is male, while the other's body characteristics are female. Not so, indicates the lab tests. These two infants, as is the case with all Siamese twins, are medically diagnosed as identical, though androgynous (at least superficially). Can we, as a culture, reach the point where we stop viewing people with only our eyes, not considering people at their core, who make life choices that suit the individual, and not the collective bias?

If the masses of humanity were to refrain from judgment based on instant "eye level" assumptions, our world's culture would operate from the perspective of oneness rather than separation. How quickly we label people and their life decisions as a monstrosity.

When someone, or something, in society appears different than would be generally expected, often the response is to step into fear and discrimination. I find it sad that many have yet to realize that our learning and progression as a soul are perfectly guided from a higher level. We summon and invite each element and experience in our daily existence for the benefit of our personal learning and ongoing soul development, as well as the advancement of humanity.

What are the key components and expansion of your spiritual perspective that you, as the reader, can gain from Rex, Roxy, and their mother's story? Within a simple foreword, I haven't the latitude to comment on each strand of Larry Bryant's tapestry intricately crafted as he calls us forward to remove our blinders and step firmly into knowing we arrive in body with purpose.

Is it so bizarre to consider that we plan each incarnation with the possibility that human suffering can, and generally does, result in a contribution to spiritual evolution? Pre-birth Rex and Roxy opted for a joint and purposeful venture, attached at the abdomen. Some souls choose a different version of an intentional joint venture by marrying in their twenties; experiencing the depth of relationship, that many never know, for 25 years; with the end result of the husband's death at age fifty, leading to ongoing telepathic communication between spouses until the demise of the wife. Were you to spend time in my office as a fly on the wall, you'd come to know this type of spousal beauty.

Past life remnants are repeatedly reflected in our life today as musical skill, tightly knit relationships, even body type and facial appearance. Without the awareness of how to label such past incarnation "bleed through," we will skip right over the bright light of soul memory that points us in the direction of knowing and mapping all that we are. From one reincarnation experience to the next, our spiritual DNA is being imprinted with impressions of: what role(s) did I play in each life?; with whom did I play these roles?; did I die young?; did my spouse or mother die young?; and a myriad of other potent experiences.

At every turn of the page, *Conjoined* is truly a beauty, as it offers the reader the opportunity to contemplate, face, and assess whether our knee-jerk, programmed societal responses may be judgmental, demonstrating a lack of awareness of our core soul-level choices that guide us with intent and purpose toward higher learning. I invite you to enjoy and examine Larry Bryant's novella as open-mindedly as possible.

Linda R. Backman, Ed.D.

Licensed Psychologist and Regression Therapist

Author of: *Bringing Your Soul to Light: Healing through Past Lives and the Time Between*

http://www.RavenHeartCenter.com

http://www.BringingYourSoultoLight.com

Prologue, by Roxanne Russell

"Isn't it better to find a new form, than cling with a perverse tenacity to the dried up and shriveled husk?"--A Victorian feminist

We, Rex and I, came into this life physically conjoined, yes--but even more conjoined spiritually.

Born on February 29, 2008, we promptly learned how unprepared we were for life on this planet. Indeed, you might say we leapt into this life, more unprepared than anyone before for its challenges and lessons.

What you're reading here amounts to my attempt to put it all into perspective, to recount a life of duality never experienced or witnessed before. For as long as nineteen years, some of you have known us as "the world's first androgynous Siamese twins," born in this "condition" by prenatal choice--and remaining so by even stronger choice.

This memoir, written by me in remembrance of us both, has a muse dating back to our early teen years--i.e., the following tanka:

> we arrived tandem,
> conjoined in body and spirit;
> we're Rex and Roxy,
> fulfilling our karmic goals--
> and looking to the future

At the age of twenty-four, our mother, Anna Mae Russell, inherited substantial wealth from her father, a widowed real estate developer in Virginia Beach, Virginia. Momma Anna, as she preferred we call her, never married. Tending to be reclusive, she nevertheless had a strong maternal instinct, which she bestowed upon two dachshunds--one male (Chou-Chou), the other female (Gem'l). Most of her social life revolved around her career as a piano teacher.

A year or so after our grandfather's funeral, our mother resolved to honor his memory by undergoing artificial insemination from an anonymous donor. Ever the risk-taker, she chose to increase the odds for successful pregnancy by taking a new fertility drug called Plutemporide. The head of the local fertility clinic had assured her that "so far, Ms. Russell, we've seen no complications whatsoever from this medication--no still births, no physical or mental deformities, no fetal predisposition toward infirmity. In fact, our records show that all the Plutemporide-facilitated babies have been exceptionally healthy, robust, and developmentally sound." Based on that professional assessment, independent-minded Momma Anna ignored the advice of her family physician, Dr. Ambrose G. Hempstead, who'd cautioned her that a multiple birth would heavily burden any single mother.

Of course, this caution from Dr. "Amby" (as we affectionately came to call him) became the ultimate understatement in our mother's case. A few months into her pregnancy, Momma Anna underwent some routine blood tests and a sonographic exam. "Yes, indeed, Ms. Russell," announced Dr. Amby, "you're gonna have a set of twins. A boy and a girl they are! A Plutemporide Special, you might say."

Just how "special" neither he nor anyone else in the medical world could imagine. From a subsequent sonogram, taken during the final trimester, the doctor discovered a slight abnormality between the two fetuses: an amorphous growth of some sort that seemed to maintain its position regardless of how we maneuvered in the uterus. This anomaly persuaded him to recommend a Cesarean-section delivery; and Momma Anna acceded.

On that 26-degree evening of February 29th, our fate would be in the hands of a skilled general practitioner who delighted in bringing life into the world, and who had performed dozens of Cesareans. Completely sedated, Momma Anna would have to wait until morning to learn what had astounded Dr. Amby and the rest of the delivery team: the mysterious growth was neither a conventional tumor nor what's known as a teratoma (such as a foot discovered growing in a newborn's brain); rather, it consisted of a nimbly, cartilaginous cord connecting me to Rex at our respective abdomens, much like the connector between the original Siamese twins, Eng and Chang.

"Could these possibly be Siamese twins?" asked Dr. Amby of his assistant, an obstetrician.

"No way," she replied. "We all know that Siamese twins always are identical, and that all identicals always have the same gender."

Frowning, Dr. Amby countered: "Well, let's run some blood tests and DNA tests tomorrow."

By mid-morning, the verdict was incontrovertible: somehow, we'd become the meat of the maxim that "one needs to see only one white crow to conclude that not all crows are black."

When the good doctor broke the news to our mother, he explained it this way: "Apparently, some sort of chemical mutation occurred from your intake of Plutemporide. Our lab tests prove that your twins are identical--not fraternal--and that they're indeed conjoined. But, don't worry--in several weeks, we'll have no difficulty in surgically separating them."

At this point, Momma Anna, still groggy from sedation, waved off the doctor with these cryptic words: "Let's discuss the need for separation later, okay?"

News of our delivery spread with the speed of the internet. Science-minded bloggers, anomaly sleuths, and religious leaders expanded the arena of astonishment and debate. We, Rex and I, had become instant public figures. To this day, I still have a clipping of the event's initial account as published in Virginia Beach's weekly newspaper, the *News Wave*. I keep it well preserved in the combination scrapbook-journal begun and maintained all these years by Momma Anna. (Incidentally, I remain grateful to Fortean researcher Larry W. Bryant's urging our mother to create and nurture her careful record of our early years.) Here's the text of the *News Wave*'s write-up:

Marvelous Mutation Produces
Male-Female Conjoined Twins

"Virginia Beach Coast Hospital officials have confirmed the birth Friday of Rex and Roxanne Russell, who have the distinction of being the world's first case of male-female Siamese twins.

"'Other than their heterology and the flexible band of sinewy fascia conjoining their abdomens, the twins appear as sound as any other set of identical twins,' said hospital spokesperson Jill Carter. She added that eventual early separation of the twins should pose no difficulty to surgeons. The male twin is conjoined at the right side of the female.

"According to Carter, medical lab tests point to the likelihood that the new fertility drug Plutemporide played a role in this one-of-a-kind genetic mutation.

"The twins' mother, Anna Mae Russell, a Beach resident in the 300 block of 35th Street, expects to bring the twins home within the next 10 days, saying that her first chore as a single mom will be how best to manage breast-feeding them."

So..."mutants" were we, eh? Oh, how so young to be labeled with such an inglamorous term! But at least it wasn't "freaks" (yet). As with all well-intentioned parents, our mother wished to shield us from much of life's harshness and despair. But she had the good sense to realize that overprotectiveness would be just as damaging, if not more so, as allowing us total free reign in our social adaptation. She certainly did have a difficult balancing act to manage; but, from today's perspective, I can't imagine any other woman, back then, who could've done it any better than she.

As you read this memoir, keep in mind that, in our yin-yang existence, Rex and I always considered ourselves as neither victims of neglect nor as any form of diabolical spawn from an even more evil mother. Rather, we viewed ourselves, as did Anna Mae Russell, as multi-lifetime voyagers, karmicly attuned to our eternal twinship.

Therefore, in tribute to both Momma Anna and Rex, I share the following tanka (composed during our turbulent teen years):

you are my brother,
Rex, my conjoined twin for life;
we're even closer
than in our previous life,
for we're soulmates forever

Chapter 1. Justifying Our Existence

"Indigo children is a New Age concept developed by Nancy Anne Tappe describing children who are alleged to possess special traits or abilities. Beliefs about indigo children range from their being the next stage in human evolution, possessing paranormal abilities such as telepathy, and lacking communication skills to the belief that they are simply more empathetic and creative than their non-indigo peers."--

wikipedia.org

In her journal, Momma Anna has documented a number of milestones in our navigating society's minefield of reaction to our presence. Here's her entry for June 29, 2008 (when we were four months old):

"I sit here, with the twins, on the waiting-room couch in Dr. Amby's office. The building's air conditioner is pumping out a breeze far too cold for the twins' (and my) comfort, so I've kept them bundled inside their custom-made stroller. As per his wont, Rex, now a few inches shorter than Roxy, is nestling his forehead against her right shoulder. As he slumbers there, she lies fully awake, as if recording all the sights and sounds of the place. A smile of contentment adorns her rosy, round face, leaving no doubt that she's become the 'dominant twin' in this union. Her bright-blond hair has a natural part in the middle, unlike her brother's, which tends to part on the left side. And, yes…their mutual hair color finds its complement in their azure irises. These, my fast-maturing 'indigo children' (as Dr. Amby dubs them), are going to need special emotional, intellectual, and physical attention, regardless of whether they remain conjoined for life.

"The office door opens to the slow entry of an elderly woman using a cane. She sits beside me and glances into the stroller.

"'Ah, twins! Are they girls or boys?'

"'One of each,' I reply.

"'Hmm . . . you're not that Russell woman who's had conjoined boy-girl twins--?'

"I interrupt her by affirming her guess: 'Yes, I am indeed . . . meet Rex and Roxanne.'

"The woman turns to me and asks: 'Aren't they overdue for separation…when is that set to happen?'

"At that moment, Dr. Amby's secretary, Dottie Johnson, calls my name; and, without answering Ms. Busybody, I spring from the couch and head the stroller toward the nurses' station."

Shortly after the preliminaries of a nurse's weighing us and checking our vital signs, Momma Anna heard a soft knock on the exam room door. Upon greeting her, Dr. Amby turned to the wall-mounted computer and entered a few update notes. Then he examined the area of our conjoinment, palpating the quasi-umbilical cord to assess its strength and resilience. (Over time, he and Momma Anna had begun referring to this connecting appendage as "the cord.")

"Well, as I explained to you last month, Ms. Russell," he began, "we still have no reason not to proceed with separation. How about scheduling it for the middle of next month?"

Our mother, our Angel of Life, had little to say except: "Can't you understand, Doctor, that my commitment as a reincarnationist won't let me interfere with the twins' karmic choice here? You can see that they're adapting quite well to their situation, so I'd rather ...--."

Dr. Amby put an arm around Momma Anna's shoulders and pleaded: "Now, you know I have nothing against reincarnationism. Have you forgotten that's how we met-during that nighttime meeting of the Karmic Research Center on Laskin Road? But shouldn't we be letting the principle of free will--*yours*, since the twins' has yet to develop--have a say here? After all, karma can affect not just the parent-choosing child but also that very parent as well."

For all his years of medical training and experience, including ample studies in medical ethics, this thirty-five-year-old physician had never dreamed of encountering such an issue as this one. The debate over abortion rights, the matter of some parents' desires to withhold blood transfusion for their critically ill children, the celebrated (and protracted) quasi-euthanasia case of the late Terri Schiavo--all seemed to him a distant cousin to the saga of Rex and Roxanne. Besides, as a recent divorce, he felt an almost romantic kinship with Momma Anna's resolve to stand by her convictions. Strong-willed women--like sirens beckoning along a tropical island's coral reefs--had always been his emotional Achilles' heel.

Without waiting for an answer from Momma Anna, Dr. Amby, content with having made a statement, eased from the room, saying, over his shoulder, "See y'all next month!"

Several weeks later, Momma Anna received a phone call from a reporter at the *News Wave*:

"Ms. Russell, the woman began, "we've received a note from someone who's identified him-/herself by the letters 'D. J.' The note has an enclosure purporting to be a photocopy of a case summary from your Dr. Hempstead."

"So, what does the note say, and what do you plan to do with it?" Momma Anna demanded.

"It says that the writer is concerned that your decision to postpone, or to permanently decline, the surgical separation of your twins amounts to child neglect or abuse...and that the writer plans to file a complaint with the city's Directorate of Child Protective Services."

"And how about the enclosure's content--what does that tell you?"

"Well, I can show all of it to you if you'd like to grant us an interview on the matter. But, mainly, the doctor's final paragraph seems to be what's ticked off this 'D. J.' person. It reads: 'Anna Mae Russell's twins appear to be adjusting well to their connectivity. But I expect that the general public--once it learns the ease by which surgery can separate them--will view their status as a form of captivity. Of their being held hostage to their mother's unconventional spiritual values. Of their being arbitrarily deprived of their pursuit-of-happiness rights."

As she moved to terminate the conversation, Momma Anna thought better of her urge to engage the reporter in a debate on the merits of surgery vs. parental prerogatives and scruples. Instead, she concluded, "I'm going to discuss this with my doctor, and I advise you not to publish anything that would invade my family's medical privacy."

Early that evening, a knock at the front door brought a round of barking from our family's ultra-protective dogs, Chou-Chou and Gem'l. Upon recognizing Dr. Amby, they trotted off to their usual location in the house's foyer.

Dressed in a nightgown and housecoat, Momma Anna seemed conflicted over the doctor's unannounced presence. On the one hand, why had he so jeopardized their doctor-patient confidentiality by putting his misgivings on written record? On the other hand, his stopping by ought to make it easier for her to plan a defense strategy.

"Oh, doc...doctor. You wouldn't believe the phone call I got from the *News Wave* this afternoon. Some reporter there got her hands on your ...--."

"Yes, I know," he said, plopping down on the floor and summoning Chou-Chou to his side. "That same reporter had called me this morning. I guess you've figured out who that 'D. J.' happens to be--my secretary, Dottie Johnson. She's promptly confessed, claiming that her conscience had driven her to this extreme."

"What happens now?"

"Obviously, Dottie's no longer my secretary. And--you've got to get a lawyer, pronto. I recommend Sol Shepherd. He has offices in both Virginia Beach and Norfolk."

Momma Anna sat down beside him. "Don't fret too much over this development, Dr. Amby." She put a hand on his as he petted Chou-Chou. Frustrated and anxious though she was, she nevertheless felt a wave of comforting empathy from this man sworn to do no harm to any patient. "If it hadn't been Dottie who did this, it eventually would've been someone else, I suppose. Would you like to have a drink?"

The doctor stood, shaking his head, "No...gotta get back to the office for some more paperwork. Please let me know if you hear anything more from that reporter." He took her hand and drew her into a cursory hug, then waved good-bye to the dogs as he departed.

Back in her second-floor bedroom, Momma Anna decided to make one more check on me and Rex. She eased open our bedroom door; through the haze of the room's nightlight, she leaned over our width-expanded crib. There, the serenity of our oneness evoked from her both a smile and a tear, her heart rhythm now coinciding with our breathing. Writing of this moment in her journal, Momma Anna realized that, in just a matter of weeks, "the cord seems to be adapting to them, rather than vice versa. In some way, somehow, my sweet little cherubs belong together, into eternity."

Dottie Johnson's egregious lapse in judgment and disregard for our family privacy included her e-mailing to the *News Wave* reporter a digital photograph of me and Rex being weighed at age four months. The photo showed us with a light towel across our groins, but the cord was entirely visible. Dottie's message declared: "See how easily, and harmlessly, we could snip this ugly thing at both ends, sew up the holes, and set these pathetic infants free!?"

Abandoning any semblance of journalistic ethics, the newspaper's editor concluded that this evidence of (alleged) parental misfeasance merited not just the intervention of local child-protective authorities but also the persuasive power of the editor's public condemnation. In less than ten days later, Dottie's photo of me and Rex accompanied an editorial titled "Deconjoin Now!"

In its summary of the case, in which the editor quoted Dr. Amby's assessment of our separability, the editorial asserted: "Remaining unseparated since birth should apply only to those Siamese-twin cases where surgical severance would patently endanger the life of either (or both)." Furthermore, the editor proclaimed that "If Dr. Hempstead refuses to facilitate separation, his license to practice medicine should be revoked immediately and permanently. Accordingly, the Virginia Beach Medical Society has begun reviewing this matter. We expect one or more volunteer surgeons to offer their skills to the director of child protective services."

As you might deduce, the *News Wave*'s editorial sparked a tsunami of reader reaction. Worldwide newswire services exported the polemic in numerous languages. Some of the cable TV networks interviewed the editor, several radio talk-show hosts weighed in with their own brand of profundity, and the *News Wave*'s online "message board" nearly crashed with the weight of public comment. Some examples:

"[From a reader named 'Concerned Parent']: How dare this Russell woman prefer that Rex and Roxanne remain permanently conjoined! I myself have twin girls, and I can't imagine how miserable they'd be if they were unable to function separately. Put this woman behind bars right now--and put those twins on the operating table next week!"

"[From 'God Fearer']: Each day these helpless infants have to struggle for the freedoms we all take for granted--the freedom to use a bathroom alone, the freedom to enjoy occasional solitude, the freedom from having to constantly confer with another person on the most elemental decisions of one's life, the freedom to sexually mature without having to look into a three-dimensional mirror, etc.--marks a form of cruel-and-unusual punishment for sins uncommitted by these two victimized infants. Deconjoin 'em now!"

"[From 'Sharpshooter']: Shame on the News Wave staff for violating the Russell family's most basic sense of decency: their medical privacy. This end-justifies-the-means mind-set should result in a court judgment against you so severe as to have your company declare bankruptcy, since you in effect already have declared *moral* bankruptcy. I'm canceling my subscription, and I plan to contribute several hundred dollars to Ms. Russell's legal defense fund."

"[From 'Mr. Justice']: Sure, Sharpshooter, go ahead and play the righteous-indignation card. But, by God, you really can't justify compelling these two defenseless babies to ruin both their emotional and physical well-being by remaining conjoined for life. This Russell woman has created a monstrosity, and she has the responsibullity [sic] to rectify it immediately. No more discussion's necessary: free R. & R., jail A.M.R.!"

"[From Anna Mae Russell]: Thank you, Sharpshooter, for your offer to help fund my legal defense. As this case gets resolved in my favor (and, indirectly, in the twins' favor), I'm prepared to win it in the Court of Public Opinion. I intend not to retreat from this responsibility as a parent and as a conduit by which Rex and Roxanne may fulfill their karmic course of life on this planet."

From all these pleadings, the one that stood out the most--especially in Momma Anna's view--came from none other than Dottie Johnson: "As the person who blew the whistle on this failure of modern medicine to properly attend to the twins' needs, I want you all to know that I won't rest until I see Rex and Roxanne strolling along the Beach's boardwalk, completely free of each other's body. To that end, I've just posted an online petition at www.petitionvoice.net; it's titled 'Help Save Rex and Roxanne!'

"As the public's electronic signatures (and supportive comments) accumulate, I'll periodically print them out and send them to the petition's three targeted recipients: the Child Protective Services, the Virginia Beach Medical Society, and the Virginia state House of Delegates Committee on Health, Welfare, and Institutions. With your prayers and God's intervention, we shall reverse this terrible injustice done unto these helpless infants."

With that manifesto, Dottie marched to the self-beating drum of conventional public sentiment. Interviews with various news/entertainment media followed. She joined the lecture circuit, speaking before civic groups, religious organizations, student bodies, and medical associations.

For her part, Dottie's nemesis--Momma Anna--chose to eschew such grandstanding. She wished to confine her public persona to known quantities of private and public support, such as the Karmic Research Center. Besides, the higher the frequency of defending herself in public, the higher the volume of hate mail arriving through our front door's mail slot (too much of which contained death threats).

Momma Anna decided to store all this noxious mail in carefully sealed file boxes, stacking them beneath a workbench in our basement. "Some day, this stuff will have much sociological value," she explained to me, years later. She almost decided to frame one of the missives; it was an undated postcard from someone named Rev. Bob Llerrem of Suffolk, Virginia. It read:

"Bitch: as a fierce opponent of abortion, I nevertheless now must concede that I would've endorsed your having aborted these horable [sic] twins from hell. Indeed, for humanity's sake, it's not too late to abort them right now. Call me at 757-[...] and I'll come over there and help you complete the job with a noose built for *two* necks. Otherwise, if I ever see those little bastard freaks unattended in your neighborhood, I intend to snatch 'em and exercise God's will single-handedly!"

On top of all that, the controversy reached the halls of Congress when Virginia's second district (Republican) Rep. C. S. W. Ford bowed to public pressure. He introduced a bill--the "Siamese-Twins Assistance, Rehabilitation, and Transmutation (START) Act of 2008"--calling for formation of "a special medical commission to address the plight of such pharmaceutical victims as Rex and Roxanne Russell. (Ironically, election campaign records showed Ford's leading the list of those Virginia solons who'd been accepting donations from the pharmaceutical industry.)

In his characterization of the bill's intent and scope, as published in the *Congressional Record*, Ford professed: "This legislation will offer comfort, funding, and other relief to those families facing tribulations similar to those of the Russell family."

However, in this historic era of economic woe, Ford's resolution gained few sponsors--thus yielding to its death by benign neglect within a House subcommittee.

Chapter 2. Summoned to Court

"I was a perfectly normal trilingual child."--Vladimir Nabokov

A few weeks after the *News Wave*'s condemnatory editorial, a piece of certified mail arrived at our house. Addressed to Momma Anna, it bore the return address of Virginia Beach's Directorate of Child Protective Services. Its two pages consisted of a "Petition to Show Cause Why the Dependent Infants Rex and Roxanne Russell Shall Not Be Remanded to the Custody of the Virginia Beach CPS Authority."

Also named as a target of the petition was Dr. Amby. After outlining the charges of child neglect/abuse and of our "possible illegal imprisonment" by Momma Anna, the document's form-letterese announced there'd be a formal hearing 30 days hence in the chambers of Judge Janet C. Emory in the Beach's Juvenile and Domestic Relations Court.

Before even reaching the end of page 2, Momma Anna squeezed the petition into a tight wad, heaving it into a corner of the foyer (where nosey little Gem'l pounced on it, thinking she'd been treated to a new toy). Momma Anna then drew a deep breath, retrieved the ball of paper, and began flattening it as she walked to the phone.

As she waited for someone to answer Dr. Amby's office number, Momma Anna noticed a slight tremble in her hands as she resumed reading the petition: "Oh, I wish he needn't be involved in all this," she said aloud. "None of it's his fau ...".

Her train of thought fizzled as she heard the doctor's voice:

"I was hoping this was you, Anna. How 'bout if I come by and take ya to lunch?"

Momma Anna, now on the living room couch, her legs curled beneath her, sighed and blurted out, "Did you get this ridiculous petition yet?"

"Did indeed. Just what I need: another meritless trip to court, eh?

"Well, you sound not too concerned. Tell me--your Norfolk lawyer, Shepherd…is that his first name?"

"Nope. His first name is Sol. And I've already made an appointment with him for tomorrow at four-thirty. Want me to pick you up at three-thirty so you can join me?"

Momma Anna managed a controlled, tepid smile: "Not only that, I want to bring the twins along with me--and to that damn hearing as well, just so everyone can see what a truly 'neglected/abused child' and its clone look like, doncha know!"

Upon hearing Momma Anna's passing on the lunch offer-- since she was facing a full load of piano students that day--Dr. Amby ended the conversation with a cheery "See ya in court, Anna Mae!"

Sol Shepherd's office, near the Gen. MacArthur Memorial, had all the accoutrements of a master practitioner in criminal defense: a wall-mounted deer's head; a cabinet display of vintage hunting rifles; a row of several antique wooden filing cabinets; a photo gallery of prominent clients pleased with his representation. Here's how Momma Anna's journal depicts the meeting:

"We arrive about 15 minutes early. The place smells of pine oil disinfectant. A manly aroma, to be sure.

"Out comes Shepherd from the toilet area. Forty-ish, toothy, and endowed with a fluffy red moustache, he quickly spies the baby stroller in which lie Rex and Roxy, wide awake.

"'Oh, please, may I hold them for a few minutes?' he pleads.

"'Why not?' I reply. He helps me scoop them up to his chest, where he clutches them as if they're both a trophy and a prized work of art.

"'These adorable little critters,' he says as they squirm a bit to get used to his bony geography. 'Look at those piercing blue eyes! Which one is the girl?'

"'The one that just dribbled on your necktie,' I answer. 'Of course, besides looking into one of them's diapers, I can take a shortcut by looking at their thighs--because Roxanne's left thigh has a one-inch-long birthmark on it.'

"He heads toward his secretary, who holds out a digital camera. 'Say, Ms. Russell, would you mind taking a couple of pictures of me with them? Please.'

"Amby chuckles at this folksy beginning of our legal relationship. As soon as I make a few snapshots, we all amble into Shepherd's conference room.

"After about twenty minutes of strategizing and discussing our (limited) options, Shepherd stands to announce that he has to visit a client in Norfolk's federal detention center at six-thirty, that he'll be mailing us a retainer agreement, and that if he loses this case, we'll owe him nothing. 'For the twins' sake,' he explains."

Over the next several days, the CPS director's general counsel issued a subpoena for all of Dr. Amby's medical records on our case. Next came the separate depositions for both Momma Anna and Dr. Amby. For her "depo session" (as she called it), our mother, boldly and proudly, brought along me and Rex. (I understand we both slept through it all.)

Now yellowing with age, the transcript of that session has this key exchange between her and the CPS counsel, a self-assured young man in his first government job:

"COUNSEL: Now, for the record, Ms. Russell, how long have you planned to keep your twins conjoined, despite the relative ease by which they can be fully surgically separated?

"RUSSELL: For as long as Nature intended for them to be conjoined, sir.

"COUNSEL: Isn't it true, madam, that you justify this permanent conjoinment by adhering to some strange notion-- based on a personal theory of reincarnational 'karma'--that these two infants, during their discarnate 'spiritual' existence, actually chose you as their mother; that they, in prebirth mode, had consulted so-called 'spirit guides' as to the most spiritually beneficial venue for their current incarnation; and that any longsuffering they might encounter from this choice can contribute to their, uh, 'spiritual evolution'?

"RUSSELL: You may characterize the notion as 'strange,' counsel; but millions of people on this planet view it as 'strange' that most of Western society has arbitrarily dismissed the available evidence for reincarnation's reality. So...-- .

"COUNSEL [interrupting]: All right, ma'am. We're here not to argue the merits of theological dogma. We're here to determine the facts of why you're resisting the surgical severance of Rex and Roxanne--wouldn't you agree?

"RUSSELL: No, indeed. I firmly disagree. I disagree with this whole process. You have no business interfering with my parenthood. You have no business treating my children as state property. You have no *damned* business invading our medical, religious, and familial privacy, period! You have no ...--".

[At this point, lawyer Shepherd signaled a time-out for our mother to leave the room and regain her composure.--R. R.]

On August 30, 2008, Judge Emory commenced the hearing. Herself the mother of an autistic teen-aged boy, she had all the intellectual and emotional resources needed to render a fair judgment. Or so advised lawyer Shepherd. And he was right. After twenty minutes of hearing from both sides, she declared a recess of thirty minutes. As she left the room, she couldn't resist leaning down to our stroller and kissing both me and Rex on the cheek.

When she reentered the room, Judge Emory was carrying a sheet of paper. It was her Memorandum of Opinion. Right behind her was a court clerk, who began to pass out copies of the document to the assembled parties and their counsel. Then-- quietly and solemnly, as if she were all too aware of the historic nature of her decision--she began reading aloud the memo's contents:

"Today, in the court's careful review of the facts, principles, and *principals*, in this case--including the various social workers' reports, witnesses' depositions, and other evidence--the court finds that the Commonwealth has failed to convince the court that its wholesale intervention at this time would be in the best interests of the twins.

"To defer to the loving, ever-attentive behavior that this mother exhibits toward her physically impaired children would be in consonance with the medical dictum of 'First, do no harm.' In the parlance of jurisprudence, this principle equates to: 'Override no parent's judgment without due cause.'

"Accordingly, the court hereby orders that respondent Anna Mae Russell appear before this court annually until the twins' sixteenth birthday, at which time the court shall order the twins' appearance to assess and establish their free-will desires vis-à-vis the status quo of their condition. In most states, the age of sixteen reflects a young person's maturity to possess a driver's license, and the court sees no reason for not applying that standard to the instant case."

In effect, the judge's ruling declared that Rex and I were a perfectly normal set of Siamese twins. That we deserved whatever autonomy that might be delegated to us by our mother. And that, along with Momma Anna, we had a confirmed (if qualified) right to be let alone.

This moderate victory over society's contrary instincts-- fueled as they were by ignorant fearfulness and/or fearful ignorance--became just another milestone in our coping with society's overall unwillingness (if not incapacity) to accept our joint venture in this lifetime.

Chapter 3. Rescuing the "Plutemporide Perverts"

"In the present day, power holds a smoother language and whomsoever it oppresses, always pretends to do so for their own good."--John Stuart Mill

When word began reaching the public that Momma Anna essentially had prevailed in court, another round of pack journalism ensued. Reporters and talk-show hosts besieged Judge Emory for interviews, which she firmly declined. Some of them backtracked, to varying degrees, from their pro-separation stance. One of these was the *News Wave*'s editor, who, in a two-hundred-word editorial, urged a moratorium on further in-depth (read: privacy-violating) coverage of "The Twins":

"We've helped create public figures out of these two children (and their mother). Having so erred, we urge our fellow media types not to journey down that same slippery slope. Let the court handle this in its reasoned discretion. Let the twins have peace from the peanut gallery!"

But crusader Dottie Johnson refused to cancel her online petition. And Rev. Bob? Well, rumors were growing that he'd resolved to redouble his efforts to rid the world of those "Plutemporide Perverts."

And he almost did.

Just a week after the court's ruling, Momma Anna was going to wheel us over to the beach's boardwalk for an after-dinner stroll. But she also wanted to lie in the waning sunlight for a while. So she asked one of her students to keep an eye on

31

us as we sat in the stroller on the front sidewalk. "I'm going back in to get the lemonade from the kitchen, Sally. I'll be right back."

Preoccupied by listening to music on her Echopod, Sally failed to notice a big SUV pulling up to the curb, its right sliding door wide open. In a matter of seconds, a bald, white man, perhaps in his early sixties, bolted out the doorway, grabbed our stroller, and shoved it (with us) into the SUV.

As the man hurried to take his seat, Chou-Chou bounded from the front porch, barking fiercely and able to sink his teeth into the man's right leg before he could close the door. The man tumbled onto the sidewalk, kicking at Chou-Chou, whose bite had torn away a portion of the man's trousers. Getting to this feet, the man started running toward Atlantic Avenue--while the vehicle's driver panicked and stepped on the accelerator.

At the moment, Momma Anna returned from inside the house. Seeing what had happened, she dropped the lemonade and screamed, "My babies! My babies! They've taken my babies!" Slumping to her knees in sheer despair, she shouted to Sally, "Call 911...call!" Sally had at least the presence of mind to use her cell phone. By this time, though, both the man on foot and the SUV had moved from sight.

A squad car arrived within fifteen minutes. The patrolman found Momma Anna in a fit of hysterics, almost convulsing at the loss of her children. Poor little Sally's efforts to calm her were fruitless. How does one comfort any mother in such a situation?

The patrolman turned to Sally and implored, "Quick . . . tell me what happened here." Sally was able to explain the event in much detail, her being a math whiz in the tenth grade: "...and then the dog made three leaps and attacked the old man, right down there at the curb--drew some blood too."

"Let's go see," said the patrolman. In the gutter, he found a strip of torn trouser, its light-green color smeared with a patch of blood about the size of a quarter. "Hmmm. This oughta prove useful to us. I wanna get it to the lab as soon as we can. He bagged the cloth and activated his radio to call for another car to pick up the bag while he stayed to fill out a report form.

Finally, Sally was managing to bring Momma Anna to her senses, saying, "It's okay now, Ms. Russell. The police tell me they're confident they're gonna find those guys."

"Please, Sally, call Dr. Hempstead's office and ask him to come here...please."

Dr. Amby's presence alone was enough to calm Momma Anna momentarily, but the jarring ring of his cell phone renewed her stress.

"It's detective Summers over at the forensic lab, Anna. [then, into the phone]: What's that, detective--you've found a DNA match for that patch of blood? Fantastic! Who is it?"

Summers revealed that the culprit was Gerald Phillip Brewer, a paroled sex offender (pedophile) now residing just several blocks away from 35th Street at a homeless shelter run by a non-denominational church. Summers continued, "We're staking out the place right now. Once we show him the evidence (including the bite wound), he'll probably confess. Then we can plea-bargain with him on the identity of the SUV driver and, eventually, discover the twins' whereabouts. I'm bettin' that, by this time tomorrow, those babies will be back home with their mother!"

Summers couldn't have been more accurate. About two o'clock the next day, Momma Anna received a phone call that began, "Well, hello thar, Bitch Russell--it's me, Reverend Bob. I'm a-givin' your freaky little bastards a nice warm bath right now. If you tell me yo' cell phone number, I'll send ya a picture of 'em. But be warned, sweetheart: it'll probably be the last one taken while they were still alive...hee, hee, hee.

"Now, then, I need some money out of you before I send these devil-spawned mutants back down deep into hell. I gotta buy me a new SUV and an airline ticket to Cool-Yo'-Heels, North Carolina, hee ...hee. So you'd better have a hundred grand ready for me by midnight tonight, or it's all over for these two younguns."

Ol' pathetic Bob didn't realize that the police already had learned his location and phone number--and that they'd already placed a tap on his landline phone. Now, he'll be facing an extortion charge as well as a double-kidnapping charge.

But the Suffolk police couldn't just bulldoze their way through his front door and hope to free Rex and me unharmed. So they concocted a ruse. They dressed up one of their women sergeants--a martial arts specialist--as a package-delivery person (the package containing a warrant for Bob's arrest, of course). Knock, knock. Door opened, suspect rendered prone in three seconds, cuffs applied within five more seconds. Search-

and-rescue team summoned. Twins found asleep on sofa pillows in Rev. Bob's bathtub.

It turned out that the (un)right reverend was one Robert Jackson Llerrem, with minimal talent for recruiting henchmen, in disguising his identity, or in downplaying his ego. He truly was a pastor, though--of the flagship facility for the very church that operated the Beach homeless shelter that was housing his accomplice.

Back home with our family and the dogs, Rex and I were too young to be adversely affected by the experience. After all, on that day when, as a two-year-old, you let your older sister feed you a couple of teaspoons of dirt from the backyard garden, did that episode leave an indelible scar upon your psyche?

Chapter 4. The Indigo Magic of Our Coming of Age

"If there really be some form of 'Heaven,' it has to be equipped with lots of pianos."--Rex Russell

Adjudged incompetent to stand trial for his heinous deeds, Robert J. Llerrem ended up spending the rest of his life in Eastern State Hospital in Williamsburg.

For his canine savvy and bravery in coming to our rescue, Chou-Chou received a good citizenship certificate from the Beach's chief of police.

Months later, Momma Anna remarked to Dr. Amby that Rex and I seemed "even more bonded to each other than ever before." She might just as well have said the same thing about her and him: they'd become lovers, spending days at a time at each other's home. They reveled in taking us with them on trips, picnics, shopping chores, and selected students' piano recitals.

For our first birthday party on February 28, 2009, Momma Anna presented each of us with a miniature, battery-powered, two-octave piano. Rex, who eventually called his new toy a "panno," seemed to display a keen ear for melody, whereas I took a more technical, harmony-prone approach to the device. Momma Anna, sensing our precocity, soon began to teach us not to rush pell-mell across the keyboard with our tiny, flailing digits. "Now, slow down, you two," she cautioned as she took Rex's piano and carefully demonstrated a couple of scales. We both turned out to be fast, eager learners; you might say that, in mind at least, we could play the piano before we could walk.

Four months later, we took our first steps as a four-legged entity, stumbling, falling once or twice, and giggling as we struggled to stay erect. Momma Anna and Dr. Amby captured this event on videotape, as she recounted in her journal:

"As usual, for such a do-it-yourself learning experience, Roxy takes the lead in helping the duo remain coordinated. We replay the videotape so that they might pick up on the nuances of stability. Then we kiss and hug them for their success, and put them back in their playpen for a rest period."

And so it went, month after month, from our acquiring one set of skills to the next. From walking sessions to "panno" practice; from ball-playing to, yes, even potty training and swimming. Momma Anna made sure that we had a customized team for our rapid development: a physical therapy coach; a home-school tutor; a visiting child psychologist; and, of course, herself as our music teacher. A few of these adults would drop by with their own children in tow, allowing us plenty of opportunity to interact with our peers. And some of Momma Anna's younger students delighted in spending post-study time with us.

In these highly structured formative years, if we'd had any unhappiness at all, it certainly had nothing to do with our eternal connectivity.

At age five, we graduated to the real instrument--a 1957-vintage Harrington studio upright, with a specially elongated bench. Just as with our regular reading prowess, we excelled in reading sheet music. In fact, Rex showed his budding talent for composing music--even to the degree of devising little pieces for our four-hand playing. Indigo-schmindigo, Rex was on the go!

We loved our real piano so much that we gave it the pet name Henry. Its base keys had the richest, longest-lasting tone we'd ever heard. It would hold its tune for many months at a time. And we came to selfishly claim it for our own, forbidding most of the other students from even touching it.

By the time we were eight, we were performing little recitals in our home. We especially liked the works of Beethoven, Chopin, and Debussy--whereby we usually had to improvise some portions because of certain natural restraints from our conjoinment. In this regard, Rex had a marvelous, nay, magical ability to emulate a given composer's compositional style.

Then, into our teen years, we'd matured enough to take our recital material to the public. Even in the milieu of musicality, however, we had to keep our guard up for the unexpected.

For example, during our very first recital--at a synagogue in Chesapeake--a front-row heckler stood up to shout, "Stop this travesty right now! These poor twins are being paraded to the public as if they were freaks in a carnival show! Get 'em to a hospital tomorrow, and cut them free!" Carrying a brand-new, serrated-blade Swiss army pocketknife, the middle-aged woman turned out to be none other than Dottie Johnson. As she was being restrained by a security guard, she shoved the unopened knife toward Rex's feet.

Grinning at all the commotion, he reached down to retrieve it, saying to me, "This'll be a fancy souvenir of our debut, right?" Thenceforth, Rex carried that knife with him every time we left home.

For our thirteenth birthday, Momma Anna and Dr. Amby drove us to Richmond for an international chamber music exhibition. We chose to stay at a hotel because of the possibility of a snowstorm that evening. A few days before that, I'd experienced my menarche. As I changed my menstrual pad to a new one, I explained the process to my wide-eyed brother: "Now, this is what Momma Anna showed me one day when she thought you were napping," I began.

"Yeah, I know the drill, Roxy. You forget that I was present--and only half asleep--when she told you."

We guffawed in unison.

Somewhere near midnight, I felt the bed shaking slightly. Rex, having turned toward me, was masturbating. As I began to shift away from him, his left hand grasped my right and guided it to his erection. He closed my fingers around his penis and, with his hand upon mine, began a pumping motion. Within a minute it was over; and, without a word, I wiped the semen upon my pajama shirt, drew him close to me, and listened to his strong breathing leveling off.

Of course, I'd felt a number of Rex's erections in the past, but this was the first time I'd helped him masturbate. (One night he'd had what I now know as a nocturnal emission, wetting a spot near the bottom of my pajamas.) Would this special night lead to any episodes of mutual masturbation? I'll let you use your own imagination on that one.

What this event may tell us all is that Dottie Johnson's and Rev. Bob's and whoever's protestations against our voluntarily remaining conjoined amounted to "protesting too much"-- projecting their own (covert) desires upon me and Rex so as to absolve themselves of any maculate tendencies.

Chapter 5. The Crucible of Adolescence

"To hear this dual prodigy, Rex and Roxanne, play their unique four-hand arrangements of works from, say, Debussy, Liszt, and Lehar is to marvel at Nature's compensatory power. Otherwise, the inescapable question persists: how much does their musicality derive from past-life exposure to such classical giants?"--From an editorial in the November 2022 issue of *Adagio* magazine

When Rex and I turned fifteen-and-a-half, our twinship incurred its most serious challenge to date. It centered on 15-year-old Vicky Saunders, a trim, blonde cheerleader whose parents, Navy officers both, recently had moved to our neighborhood from Pensacola, Florida.

We first met Vicky at the little drugstore near the corner of Atlantic and 35th. She'd gone there to pick up some treats for her poodle.

"Oh," said I as we stood in line at the checkout counter, "I see you have a dog, too. We have a couple of dachshunds. They're getting quite old now, but they still love those treats. "As we exchanged names, Rex dropped a couple of quarters and stooped down to retrieve them, causing me to stoop simultaneously, of course.

Catching a glimpse of the cord, Vicky said, "Hmmm . . . y'all must be those conjoined twins my mother was telling me about. I've never met a celebrity before. Imagine this: I'll be living on the same street as yours. Any chance we'll end up in some of the same classes?"

"Well," Rex chimed in, "we have our own set of tutors who teach us at home. I guess you might say we're too much of a distraction to attend public school."

"And," I added, "at home we can use any bathroom we please without causing a *major* distraction to others."

The three of us chuckled over that touchy fact of conjoined life, Vicky clicking her heels together in a moment of come-to-attention awareness.

It took us just a matter of days before we became good friends. We played cards together that summer, spent plenty of time at the beach, and even read books together. Vicky had a knack for draftsmanship and math, mentioning that she hoped to become an architect. Not musically inclined herself, she did, however, love to sit and watch Rex and me practice. She was developing a crush on Rex--and he knew it.

By summer's end, Vicky and Rex seemed almost as inseparable as Rex and I.

And that solemn realization became the Great Sticking Point.

On a Saturday evening in early September, we three were attending an outdoor music festival at the boardwalk. As a local band played one of Madonna's pop tunes--"Crazy for You"-- Vicky grabbed Rex by his right shoulder, drew close to him, and began dancing. Oblivious to the awkwardness of this gesture, Rex obliged by shuffling a few steps, then stopping to kiss her. Addled adolescence was asserting itself for all to see, and Rex was its usher.

Later that night, as we lay in bed, I quizzed Rex about the practicality of having a serious girlfriend. "How's this gonna work?" I asked. Is Vicky just trying to tease us?"

"What do you mean--'*us*,' Roxy? She's just showing her affection to *me*, that's all. She's made it clear that she fully accepts me, even though I'm tied to you."

Rex's voice, tinged with irritation and sarcasm, caught me off guard; and I shifted as far to the left as I could, uttering not another word. Rex fell asleep within a few minutes, but it seemed like an hour before I followed suit. A rift was occurring, and I felt I had no power to stop its growth.

During practice the next morning, Rex told me he wanted to take a thirty-minute break to begin composing a right-hand-only arabesque in honor of Vicky's upcoming sixteenth birthday. In an effort to suppress my mounting pangs of jealousy, I asked, "Would you like for me to add some left-hand harmony to it? We could title it 'Vive Vicky!'"

Of course, Rex, in his tendency toward introspection, had no difficulty in detecting my semisuppressed sarcasm. Now on the defensive, he sighed: "Look, Roxy, I've already told ya that Vicky poses no threat to you, to me, or to US. She simply wants to share, in a more intimate way, part of her life with me--and I certainly want her to do so. Why can't you adjust to that?"

"I'm afraid, that's all. You know that cliché about 'three's a crowd'? Whether Vicky--or you--acknowledges it or not, her regular presence here is becoming divisive."

"So...what do you want from *me*, Roxy?"

I curled my right arm around his abdomen as I clutched his left hand with mine. Looking straight at his face, with my tears welling up and about to spill over, I replied: "I want you to tell Vicky to, basically, withdraw from our life--that's all."

Rex shoved my hand and arm away from him. "Well, I'll tell her no such thing, damn it! In fact, I'll call her right now and tell her how much I love her and need her to spend the night with *me*!" He reached for the cell phone resting on the upper ledge of the piano.

I panicked. "No!" I shouted as I knocked the phone from his hand and against the wall, shattering its casing. My tears gave way to sobs. "I won't let her ruin our life!"

Consumed by anger and a degree of humiliation, Rex reacted out of desperation. Shouting "I'm gonna determine what's best for *my* own life--right now!" he grabbed his open-bladed Swiss army knife, which he'd been using to sharpen a red-pigmented pencil. With one swipe of the blade, he inflicted a two-inch-long, quarter-inch-deep wound upon the cord. We both let out a scream (his being less intense than mine) as the pain ran its course and as the odor of blood reached our nostrils.

By this time, Momma Anna had entered the room to determine what all the fuss was about. Upon seeing the steady flow of blood staining our clothes, she, too, began to scream: "What has happened...what has happened here!?"

Before I could begin to explain, Dr. Amby, who'd been helping prepare our lunch, rushed in to take charge. He quickly diagnosed that the cut had severed no major veins--and that several stitches, some antibiotic ointment, a stabilizing bandage, and some pain medication would remedy the physical situation. As to our emotional state, he and Momma Anna both agreed that we all could benefit from an indefinite moratorium on further contact with Miss Vicky Saunders. That night, as Rex and I entered into a deep, drug-facilitated sleep, Momma Anna phoned Vicky's mother to plead for a hiatus, the latter being in full agreement.

From Momma Anna's journal: "How lucky I am to have Mrs. Saunders's understanding and sympathy. I of course wish I could've foreseen this crisis, but I'm still learning--too often by trial-and-error, alas--how to cope with the twins' special needs. Amby suggests that I schedule some psychotherapy sessions for them as they near their court-imposed deadline for self-determination. But I have an alternative course of action. Tomorrow, I'm going to ask Amby to hypnotically regress either Rex or Roxanne (or both) to their lifetimes immediately preceding their current one. The insight we may gain from that exploration might help us all come to terms with their karmic debts/goals and with their further exercise of free will."

Chapter 6. A Reincarnational Reckoning

"Our writers and poets find the meaning, or hidden life, in the observable life; they elicit from the visible what is invisible--who we are and where we are going and to what moral consequence."--E. L. Doctorow

Sitting in a chair across from me and Rex, while we and Dr. Amby shared the living room couch, Momma Anna fiddled with the settings of a tripod-mounted video camera (the one she'd normally use to record a recital). We could sense her agitation about this inner look at our joint souldom.

"Okay," she said, with a forced smile. "All set for action! I'll try to relax...so y'all too can relax."

In his most fatherly manner, Dr. Amby explained the process, activated our slow-ticking metronome at the coffee table, and began the session with a soothing stream of assurances and commands:

"Now, close your eyes, relax your muscles, and visualize that you're walking along the shore of a lake, where you feel at peace with nature and wish to linger there indefinitely. That's right: breathe easily and deeply. As you listen for the motion of the lake's waves, you feel sleepy and decide to lie upon the grassy hillside. Now, either or both of you choose to take a nap. As I count from five to zero, you'll fall into a deep sleep but still will hear my voice and wish to follow my instructions. One - two - three...".

I opened my eyes and looked at Dr. Amby. As I started to speak, he put a finger to his lips, shook his head, and switched off the metronome. He realized that I wasn't going to be an easy hypnotic subject. He pointed to Rex, who, obviously, already had entered a deep trance. For the rest of the session, Dr. Amby concentrated on regressing Rex--first, via earlier stages of youth amidst the current lifetime, then through suggestion, on the count of five, into the immediately preceding life experience.

When he came to "five," Dr. Amby instructed Rex to select a particularly pivotal segment of that previous life to recount. "Tell me, now, Rex, where you are in this past period of existence, what your name is there, what you're doing, and why you're doing it and with whom."

From the transcript made from the videotape, we have this revelation:

REX: We're in Dresden, near the end of World War Two.

DR. AMBY: Do you mean Dresden, Germany? And are you a German citizen?

REX: Yes. My name is Marta, and I'm running, furiously, with my husband, Fritz Holtzmann.

DR. AMBY: Do you know whether the soul of this person--uh, Fritz--now has a role in your twenty-first-century life of Rex Russell?

REX-AS-MARTA: Yes. Fritz, in year 2008, became my sister, Roxanne.

[Here, Dr. Amby noticed that Rex's breathing had become labored, his face flushed, his eyes squinted.]

DR. AMBY: I want you to calm yourself, Rex--so that you can continue with your account.

REX-AS-MARTA: We've stopped running. We're resting on the steps of the local post office. It's nighttime, but the British bombers keep crisscrossing the city, dumping their fire bombs at will throughout the population centers. It seems that the post office is the only building not in flames...[gasping].

DR. AMBY: What are you and Fritz carrying with you?

REX-AS-MARTA: I have my violin, and Fritz has his viola. We were just heading home from practice with our chamber music group when the firebombing started. Now, we hardly can breathe, and the hot air reeks of fumes from spent explosives, burning flesh, boiling blood. I'm pleading with Fritz to resume our flight--we have only about two more kilometers before we can reach our apartment. "No!" he's shouting. "The post office has more stone structure than most other buildings. We might be all right if we can make it into the basement." I beg him: "let's leave our instruments inside, then. But home is where we belong!"

[Dr. Amby once again noticed how Rex's body was tensing from the stress of reliving this trauma, and told him, "Try to relax a bit more, Rex, but do keep telling what's happening to Marta and Fritz.]

REX-AS-MARTA [almost impatiently]: We're striking out again, tightly holding hands in the dim, orangey light as we step across dead or dying bodies, and dodge falling debris. I whimper to my husband, "Don't ever let go of me, Fritz!" As we near the perimeter of a small park across from our apartment building, whose rooftop now is spouting flames, Fritz slips upon a pile of broken glass, sustaining a severely broken left ankle and a deep gash on his left thigh.

DR. AMBY: Do the size and location of that gash correspond to the dimensions of the slim, arrow-shaped birthmark on Roxanne's left thigh today?

REX-AS-MARTA: Yes, they do. Precisely.

[Sensing there'd be a disastrous end to the account, Dr. Amby urged Rex to maintain a detached, observational view of the ensuing events. "View the scene as if you were looking down upon it from a relatively cool, safe observation tower, Rex."]

REX-AS-MARTA [now choking mildly as if trying to clear his lungs of heat and smoke]: I just know we're both going to die in that place. But I try to keep Fritz alive. I leave him on the sidewalk, yelling back to him, "There's a wheelchair in our lobby. I'll go get it for you." Protesting, he begs me not to go inside: "Stay with me, my darling--just for a little while longer!" I break free of him and enter the darkened building, groping my way among the lobby's furniture. Though unable to locate the chair, I do find a broom, thinking that Fritz could use it as a crutch.

[At that moment in the session, Dr. Amby, noticing my tearful eyes and blanched face, hugged my shoulders and whispered to me, "Just a few more minutes, Roxy."]

DR. AMBY [interrupting Rex]: I can imagine how this must pain your soul to be reliving such an ordeal, Rex. And I admire your stamina in staying with it. Just a few more minutes and the pain will subside and I'll bring you back to your home in Virginia.]

REX-AS-MARTA: I can sense the end coming. With the broom in my hand, I turn back toward the front door. Before I can take a step forward, a ceiling beam, loosened from its moorings by the bomb blast, comes crashing down upon my shoulders. I stumble up to the doorway, from where I barely can see Fritz holding out his arms and crying for me: "Marta, Marta...please come back!" Choking back my own sobs, I move forward but trip upon an overturned suitcase, striking my head upon the foyer's stone threshold. That skull-shattering blow causes my death.

DR. AMBY: And what about your husband's fate?

REX-AS-MARTA: Shortly afterwards, Fritz dies from shock and asphyxia; thereafter, we experience our souls' reuniting with our soul group.

Most reincarnationists would find it easy to associate the close connectivity of Dresden's Marta and Fritz to today's Rex and Roxanne. The days and weeks after this hypnotherapeutic session--in which our family (by which term we of course include Dr. Amby) watched and rewatched the taperecording-- brought us ample opportunity to weigh and interpret the Rex-as-Marta account. Its cathartic content doubled in value when we showed it at a meeting of selected members from the Karmic Research Center. These experts' consensus left little doubt that our case--

--Reconfirms the reality of reincarnation (e.g., certain--albeit minimal--surviving historical material reveals the former existence of the then-world-famous musical team of Fritz and Marta Holtzmann);

--Accounts for the musical precocity of the Rex-Roxanne musical team; and

--Illuminates the karmic logic behind our souls' mutual choice of planet, parent, conjoinment, and an evolutionary path forged by physical bodies (each with an autonomous mind that just happens to host a spiritual entity some folks like to call "the soul").

Armed with that extent of esotericism (though mild for this day and age), it wasn't long before we had to summon it for our defense in still another legal challenge to our joint venture upon Earthly life.

Chapter 7. How Do You Punish One Siamese Twin for the Misbehavior of the Other?

"If they had to be put together, I think they were put together perfectly."--Patty Hensel, mother of the two-headed girl named Abigail and Brittany (circa 1997)

By the end of October, our family secret had leaked to the public. Rex suspected that Vicky, in her aim to retaliate against me (if not against Rex) for their disaffection, had spread word among her friends that Rex had maliciously attacked me with a knife.

Eventually, the indefatigable Dottie Johnson learned of the incident. According to family court records, she demanded that the Child Protective Services investigate and bring all necessary criminal charges against Rex. She in effect was setting up a Hobson's choice for the court: if you send Rex to prison, how can you in good conscience send him there without surgically separating the two of us?

On the strength of Dottie's intervention, Judge Emory convened a short hearing in her chambers. Subpoenaed for the occasion were complainant Dottie and defendants Rex (with me), Momma Anna, and Dr. Amby. Also attending were the case's original (and now senior) CPS counsel and, of course, Momma Anna's lawyer, Sol Shepherd.

And, once again, the CPS legal office had subpoenaed Dr. Amby's medical records on our case. These included his report on the knife incident, plus the transcript of his hypnotherapy session with Rex.

As the CPS counsel, smug in his prosecutorial role for promptly resolving this matter, began to characterize us as a "simple yet bizarre case of familial dysfunction," Momma Anna set down some notes for her journal. Here's an excerpt:

"This CPS guy obviously cares more about his winning this case than he does about the twins' welfare. And I think Judge Emory sees right through his arrogance. What's this?--he's telling her that the record clearly shows Rex has committed domestic abuse and that she has no choice but to order immediate separation. He says that if I fail to cooperate, then the twins should be turned over to CPS custody. But Emory interrupts him by gesturing to lawyer Shepherd, who responds:

"'Your honor, now that Rex and Roxanne are nearly sixteen, it would behoove us all if we were to accede to *their* wishes as much as possible--rather than to accept the arbitrary expedience advocated by the complainant and the CPS intervenors. I therefore would like to pose a question or two to the twins themselves...'.

"Emory smiles and looks directly at Rex and Roxy: 'Proceed, counselor.'

"Sol faces Rex and asks, 'Do you, Rex, view your sister as an expendable appendage--be she a physical one, an intellectual or emotional one, or some combination thereof?'

"Rex grasps Roxy's right hand and replies, 'You've said the key word, sir--"sister." As *twin* siblings, we've come to know--almost intuitively--that what's generally good for one of us applies equally as well to the other. We have no ambiguity about that. Of course, that equation never has ruled out our--often unconsciously--negotiated exercise of free will.'

"Upon hearing this, Dottie Johnson exudes a sigh of frustration. Then Roxy chimes in: 'Mr. Shepherd, I can tell you right now that Rex never has had any intent to harm me. True, that knife incident arose from an argument, but neither of us, at the time or right now, considers it a malicious assault on me. As the so-called "victim" in all this, I, upon my own free will, refuse to press *any* charges against my brother, my mother, or Dr. Amby. And I'm asking the court to dismiss this intrusion right now.'

"By this time, Judge Emory has read--and heard--enough about this protracted case. She declares: 'Once again, the commonwealth has exceeded its familial-oversight authority in this matter. I caution the agency not to repeat such poor judgment in the future. What's more, I order that the agency reimburse the defendants' attorney's fees, that the agency keep all its related records sealed from public view until the twins reach age eighteen, and that this case be dismissed upon my written order. Rex and Roxanne...please depart this courtroom in peace and security--and continue pursuing your life's purpose and desires unencumbered by external pressures.'

"With that, Emory removes her robe, comes to the opposite side of the room, and shakes my family's hands in a gesture of solidarity."

Momma Anna's journal went on to describe Dottie's despair, the chagrin of the CPS counsel, and her own elation over our having been vindicated. When we returned home that afternoon, we sensed a bit of perplexity from Chou-Chou and

Gem'l over our exuberance at this early birthday present for Rex and me.

Chapter 8. A Storm of Transition

"The poet C. K. Williams came to Missoula some years ago and spoke of 'narrative dysfunction' as a prime part of mental illness in our time. Many of us, he said, lose track of the story of ourselves, the story which tells us who we are supposed to be and how we are supposed to act."--William Kittredge (From "The Politics of Storytelling")

A week after Judge Emory's hearing, Momma Anna received a piece of mail from the courthouse. The envelope contained a photocopy of Emory's order, to which the judge had stapled a hand-written note "To the Russell Family."

"Please notice," it began, "that, because last week's hearing occurred so close to the twins' sixteenth birthday, it no longer will be necessary to hold any further status-update sessions about your compliance with the court's initial order in this matter. The enclosed order therefore supersedes the initial one. I take great pleasure in knowing that this modification will help you all get on with your lives! -- J. C. E."

During the subsequent three years since that note's delivery--in which Rex and I seemed to thrive in our musical career and throughout our interaction with the general public--we, the Plutemporide polymorphs" (as one social critic labeled us), had few developmental difficulties. As always, we credited this stability to both Momma Anna's and Dr. Amby's wise and supportive parenting. Also within those three years, our two "other siblings," as we called them (Chou-Chou and Gem'l), succumbed to old age, their cremains now buried near the tool shed in our back yard.

Our early exposure to the doctrinal aspects of reincarnation had afforded us a more detached view of dying/death/grief than was customary in Virginia's staid southeast region. Even so, the loss of those two dogs cut to our very souls. For, somehow, they had perceived our specialness; had adapted quickly and fully to it without any hint of fear, doubt, pity, or disdain. In our eyes, that unconditional acceptance--and their protectiveness as to our innate vulnerability--made *them* far more-special creatures than we'd ever been. We could only hope that, for humankind's sake, dogs, cats, and other pets experience some form of reincarnation.

Some people visit Virginia Beach because of the legend that its ocean-affected atmosphere has holistic-healing properties. (Perhaps that's why Chou-Chou and Gem'l managed to live so long.) Others come here to seek out its wealth of alternative spirituality. Notice that I say "spirituality" rather than religiosity (though, as you've seen from this memoir, there's plenty of the latter hereabouts).

Occasionally, a visitor will explain that she has come here to examine "the legacy of the Yin-and-Yang Twins." Lately, the flow of these spiritual seekers has increased, offering their camaraderie, their empathy, their solace.

Yes...their solace--upon hearing the news that has changed my life forever. The event in question began near noon on April 5, 2027.

Rex and I were polishing the last several bars of an etude that he'd begun composing on our nineteenth birthday. "I'm thirsty," he said. "Let's break for some more lemonade."

"You look tired, Rex. Do you want to take a nap?"

Without answering, Rex put his right palm to his forehead. Then, saying something about a "pain in my head," he lurched backward, the weight of his body pulling us from the piano bench to the floor.

Momentarily dazed from the fall's impact, I lay there, uttering not a word. Glancing at Rex's now-ashen face, I noticed a stream of blood pouring from his nose and mouth. Within seconds, his eyes closed and his body convulsed. I screamed in terror. Instinctively, I knew Rex had died. Nothing had prepared me for this eventuality. Hysterics overwhelmed me. I was unable to help my brother--and, at that moment, I seemingly was even more powerless to help myself. The mix of grief and fear had emotionally paralyzed me.

Momma Anna was out at the grocery store, and not due home for another hour or two. Dr. Amby, however, then on the back-porch deck, heard my cries and rushed to my side.

I shouted, "Rex! Rex!--help him!"

Quickly, Dr. Amby turned to check Rex's pulse. On finding none, he clutched his cell phone and dialed 911.

"Rex is dead, Roxy," my de facto father told me, the tenseness of his facial muscles betraying his otherwise professional composure. "We've got to get you separated quickly! Here, let me use my belt as a tourniquet."

I stretched away from Rex as far as the cord would allow. Then Dr. Amby wound his elastic belt around the cord and tied it firmly in place as if he were tying off an infant's umbilical cord.

"I've asked for two ambulances, Roxy. One for each of you. As soon as we sever the cord, one of the ambulances will take you and me to the hospital, where we'll finish the operation, okay?"

We both tried to smile so as to convey mutual reassurance, but the gravity of the situation wouldn't have it. Now that Rex's heart had stopped beating, the flow of his blood was slowing somewhat, but Dr. Amby was concerned that some of Rex's deoxygenated blood would contaminate my system. (Already, I was hyperventilating and (I thought at the time) was experiencing shortness of breath.)

"Is that a siren I hear now, Dr. Am...--?"

"Yes, it is, honey--the first ambulance is arriving right now. Hold on while I go let in the crew."

He bounded for the front door, opened it, and shouted to the disembarked driver, "Hurry, guys--bring one stretcher, some oxygen, a blanket, a scalpel kit, and some local anesthetic!"

Amazed at the sight before them, the disaster-hardened crew nevertheless diligently and efficiently followed Dr. Amby's instructions, first hooking me up to an oxygen tank, next using the blanket to cover most of Rex's body, and then anesthetizing my end of the cord. The anesthetic injection took about ten minutes to take effect, and Dr. Amby took only another fifteen to do the severance. Just as he completed the closing-off of the artery-like central vein at the cord's midsection, the second ambulance arrived.

Obeying Dr. Amby, the second crew removed Rex's body for transport to the hospital's morgue. One of the crewmen volunteered to stay behind and clean up the blood spillage--and to await Momma Anna's possible arrival. Dr. Amby told him, "Thank you for this extra effort, sir. As soon as we arrive at the hospital, I'll call Ms. Russell at her cell number and ask her to meet me there."

En route to the emergency room, Dr. Amby told me that he had no doubt that Rex had incurred rupture of a cerebral aneurysm. "I wonder," he said later, "if Rex had had a propensity for that condition because of his prior lifetime as Marta, who you'll recall died from a crushed skull."

"Well, he used to get headaches far more often than I, Dr. Amby."

The E. R. staff determined that Dr. Amby's work had been nearly complete, that I needed no blood transfusion, and that I should be going home in a few days, wearing several internal/external stitches and due for minimal scarring.

While she naturally was devastated by Rex's death, Momma Anna felt comforted by my survival. You might say she now was experiencing a new level of the yin-yang motif: her (dark) loss of one child but her (bright) retention of his clone.

Several days later, we buried Rex's cremains next to those of Chou-Chou and Gem'l. On the engraved river stone, his epitaph reads: "The Music of His Spirit Lives On."

Epilogue

"You see, fantasy is not an escape out of anything, it's an escape into something."--Fantasy painter (and twin) Greg Hildebrandt

Now at age twenty-five (the same age, by the way, at which Momma Anna had given birth to Rex and me), I await the birth of this memoir in print. If it undergoes as much publishers' rejection as, say, Richard Bach's Jonathan Livingston Seagull but yet manages to become published, I shall feel honored. For I do realize that, in the United States at least, the theory of reincarnation probably will remain mythicized and/or marginalized amidst the larger society. Even so, any Western publisher daring to elevate reincarnational study/discourse to practical levels of wide acceptance deserves every penny you've spent to own your copy of this book.

In her handbook *Write the Story of Your Life*, the late Ruth Kanin, Ph.D., observed that "If there is such a thing as true autobiography, it is this: that you allow us a glimpse of your soul, even if you present a fragment of your life."

Fragmentary though it be, this account of my tandem journey through life with my clone (Rex) fits the numinous mold for what Kanin had gleaned from the pioneering work of psychologist O. Hobart Mowrer. She cited his "argument for the restoration of exomologesis, a theological term found only in unabridged dictionaries: 'complete openness about one's life, past and present, to be followed by important personal change, with the support and encouragement of other members of the "congregation."'" In the case of me and Rex, the good folks at the Karmic Research Center have served as the "congregation."

65

Hence, you now hold in your hands a modern specimen of an exomologetic memoir, especially as regards its reincarnational leitmotiv.

In their tutorial *Important Words: A Book for Poets and Writers*, the writer-teacher team of Bill Brown and Malcolm Glass notes that "A writer's most important job is to find (not invent, but discover through the process of writing) how and why a subject matters." That kernel of wisdom applies to all forms of creative writing, from fiction and poetry to essays and memoir--the latter especially in my case, where my own discovery unfolds almost concurrently with yours.

In the realm of "Where Are They Now?" I can tell you that--

--Momma Anna and I, along with Dr. Amby, still live in our home in Virginia Beach.

--I recently met Dottie Johnson as I and my steady boyfriend, Erik, were strolling along the boardwalk. She burst into tears when she recognized me, declaring: "Ever since you lost Rex, I've wanted to visit you to apologize for my narrow-mindedness, but I was afraid you'd never forgive me! Now, I don't care if you do withhold forgiveness--I simply must let you know how much I regret intruding into you life." I of course, by a kiss upon her cheek, did express my total forgiveness.

--The Karmic Research Center has dedicated its musical library to the memory of Rex Russell. You'll find there copies of his published scores, CD/DVD recordings of some of our recitals, and videotaped excerpts from a few of our family outings.

--Henry--our venerable upright "panno"--still is getting a daily workout from my hands.

--Now-retired Judge Emory plans to buy copies of this book for some of her relatives and friends.

--Vicky Saunders, currently living with her husband in San Diego, keeps in regular e-mail contact with me.

--The outfit that had created Plutemporide (Pregnassist, Inc.) was facing so many liability claims that it recently had to file for bankruptcy. (Before that downturn, the drug itself had undergone reformulation so as to help rare zoo animals reproduce with more ease and regularity.)

Otherwise, dear reader, thank you for reading our story -- and for any decision you may make to advance the principle that reincarnation remains not a curse but an opportunity. Seize it...and continue evolving within the ranks of the *spiritually* conjoined!

R. R., Va. Beach (2030)

LaVergne, TN USA
29 July 2010
191289LV00002B/1/P